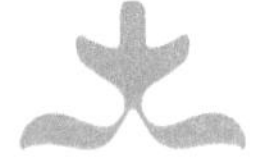

THE 75% MAN

The Living Solution Bonus Book

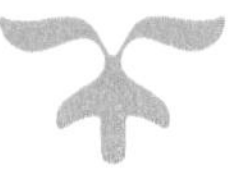

Paul Posey Sr.

The 75% Man

and

The Living Solution

Contact Me

Please follow me:

Facebook: **bit.ly/NEG2POSSpeaks**

Instagram: **Neg_2_Pos**

Email: NEG2POS@outlook.com

I'm available for public speaking, inspirational events, and family workshops. To schedule a date, contact me.

TABLE OF CONTENTS

Preface ix

The Creation 1

The Eyes of a Boy 3

Deciphering the Past 7

The Product of Man 11

The Man in Me 13

What is a Real Man? 15

What is Whole? 23

Recognize where you come from 24

Acknowledge how you feel today 25

Do something about it 26

Redefine your life 27

The Beginning 29

THE 75% MAN

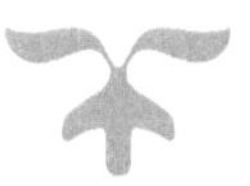

PREFACE

My head spins every time I read a quote or post about "being a real man." We argue about our opinions and fight over facts and feelings about the subject. Women are so angry about our shortcomings as men. They are unaware that their words are slicing the readers like paper cuts. We cringe when we hear the disdain in their voices as they tell their hurtful tales of how a man neglected their feelings and trampled on their hearts. I want to scream at the top of my lungs, "WE DON'T KNOW WHAT WE ARE DOING!"

The truth of the matter is that you are picking us way too soon; we are not 100% of the men we can be yet. You pick us based on potential and hope and a whole bunch of "how it should be." The worst part is that collectively, you barely stop to notice that you are hurting that overgrown boy twice as much. We cannot be broken if we were never whole.

In this book, I will share my view of what has seen swirling around in my head for the last two months. See,

I just recently hit 75% on my way to a solid 100% of the man I could be.

My Disclaimer:

I am no scholar; I will not hit you with a bunch of stats because I have been on this earth for a half-century. You can learn a lot in fifty years if you live with the idea.

"Live to learn, learn to live; that's how you get to peace." N2P

"Never apologize for the truth. That would be living a lie."

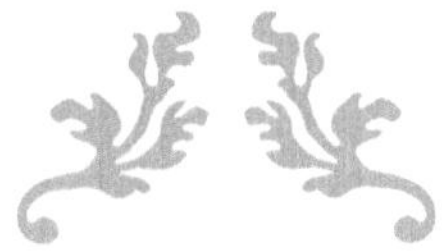

THE CREATION

It's hard to hear story after story of how we came about as children. There are only a handful of us who were planned. The rest were created through various other avenues—premature sexual encounters, drunken mishaps, the game "hide and go get it," and those who confuse sex with love. I'm not going to leave out the rape, incest, and molestation, which are very real. Of course, our fallback is that it was a part of some divine plan and all of it was supposed to be. However, our ignorance was not bliss because we knew a new life was being made. We have been making babies for hundreds of years. So, stop bullshitting the child when they finally ask you the questions, "How did I get here?" or "Why did you have me?"

We are rarely honest in sharing our shame with our children. I'm not sure how we think we are sparing them some type of heartache by not telling the truth.

It is the flaws of parents that narrow the wide road of mistakes for our children. We are the "Champions of

Mistakes," the "Masters of Mayhem," and we were truly not angel-like during the process of becoming parents.

You are responsible for everything you create, on purpose, by mistake, or by divine plan. Most of us are truly repeating the same patterns and roads our parents traveled.

The big question should be, "Why are we still living the same hurtful cycles over and over again?"

In recent years, I've started to see that some are trying to make a difference for the children of tomorrow, and it's about time. We need to understand that we are tomorrow's history and that our work has just begun. We are in charge of the trends and traditions the children of tomorrow will live by when they become parents.

THE EYES OF A BOY

Boys want to be men; we want to be our dads, granddads, and uncles. Our instincts are to repeat the things we see and hear from them. Watching a man walk, talk, protect, provide, solve problems, and achieve goals is just a short list of the traits we need and want to see modeled. We want to feel loved, heard, taught, and disciplined to be ready to fulfill our roles like the men before us. We need to see a man battle life's unnecessary tyrants and be a leader for his family.

As a boy, those were the things I only saw glimpses of from other dads. This was not so in my house; my mother was the breadwinner, protector, disciplinarian, and provider. Somehow, deep in my head, I knew something was off, but I could not put my finger on it until much later in life.

I understand that what you model in front of your child is likely what they will do. Do not fool yourself into thinking that is not so. From cussing to smoking, fighting, and many more negative things, they will do what they see. Yes, there are some positives as well, but positive things do not put you in jail or in harm's way.

Can you honestly say that you wanted your child to have it better than you did and that you intentionally modeled the life you wanted them to have? Or, did you give them stuff and model little or nothing for them to build on and form their character? If you brag about how spoiled he is or was, how has that enhanced his life as an adult? ***"Spoiled" means "rotten."***

Modeling appropriate behavior for a boy is important in all aspects of life, from cutting the grass to going to work, giving them their own tools to fix things, and even dating, and most importantly, how to love someone in a relationship. When you leave things out, they are slow to grow in those areas. You know this because you were a child before, and you grew to find out what was not on the list of lessons your parents passed down to you. In turn, you had to learn many lessons the hard way.

How does telling boys they should not cry or show emotions and modeling horrific abusive relationships in front of them help? For the record, holding off on displaying relationships at all doesn't really help.

When we send our children out into the world unarmed, we are not doing them any favors. Your life is their classroom. You are the teacher, the principal, and sometimes the janitor as well. It is your job to clean up the messes sometimes.

Our tears and anger are often from finding out we have been miseducated. You may not get your report card as a parent until your children are in their early twenties. Then you either ignore the role you played in their upbringing or blame your parents for giving you the tools you passed down.

"We did the best with what we had" is the slogan for parents who did the bare minimum—sad, but true.

If it is true that you never stop being a parent, then every day you breathe, you have a chance to improve something. So, after that statement, you obviously know there is room for change.

DECIPHERING THE PAST

There will come a time in your boy's or man's life when he will realize he did not get everything he needed while in your home. Quite often, it shows in their relationships with other people. It is frustrating and embarrassing to say, "I do not know," "I don't know how," "no one ever told me," and the classic, "no one ever showed me." Your child is not lying to you; they are deeply hurt by you.

When a young man chooses a woman whose father has taught her more than he will ever know, his knowledge is called into question. He will have to be open to being taught by her on the spot, which could lead to some type of resentment, or he will have to seek help from another man to learn something new, and pride can produce another hurdle.

My mother showed me many things. For the most

part, I knew how to do things that people would say were manly. However, what I needed were tools to unite, lead, and love my family, and I didn't have them. It took years and many, many mistakes to figure out why it was that way. In our love for our parents, we do not question them while we are in "Life School." We also do not come with a list of lessons that we are going to need before we venture out into the world. Hmm, maybe if we had a school counselor pick the classes we needed as children in our personal lives, we would have a better shot at living, and not just surviving, life's journey.

It took me forty-three years, a divorce, and many children to understand that I knew very little about love, receiving it, projecting it, and having a full range of emotions. Those things were dampened as a boy. It took some soul-searching and reflection on my life to see this. My mother stifled me from asking questions about her upbringing—why this and why that. She refused to openly show emotions.

If you haven't figured it out yet, we are programmed to only upgrade our lives after something bad has happened, such as a loss of life.

This is when our need for answers comes to haunt our parents. We must take them on a journey back to creation. Most parents are good at trying to bury their shame and will almost kill the child inside to keep it buried. Even worse is to hit your child over the head with it for years by degrading the choices you made in a partner that brought them into this world. "I can't stand your daddy," or "he is dead to me."

Your immediate past is something that truly needs to be studied, way before you think about doing a DNA test to see if your great, great, great grandparents were royalty. Because your parents have walked in your shoes, they should have some insight into the pitfalls and traps that are right outside the front door, right where they placed your luggage. I would like to say that the conversation your children are asking for is not about you; it's their personal curiosity and a part of their growth. If you never want to have that gut-wrenching conversation, be the best parent you can be, not the parent with the most hidden history.

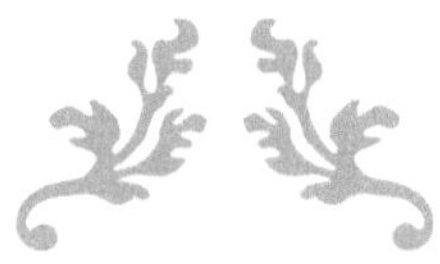

THE PRODUCT OF MAN

The sons you raise are the men of tomorrow. Let this sink in, because some women are screaming to the heavens, "Where are these men coming from?" Some men have no concept of love or providing; they have violent tendencies; they are unaccountable and sometimes just disrespectful. Look left and right; you are the creators of the children you are looking at. Doing the best with what you have cannot always be the go-to statement anymore.

For those of us between forty and fifty, we are just now understanding that we must unpack and sift our past to move forward in life or just have peace of mind. Do you mean to tell me that you want your children to experience unnecessary pains and lessons that you could have shared, like having their car repossessed, having bad credit, having to pay rent, being homeless, being jobless, sofa surfing, using drugs or alcohol, and overall foolery that we have already experienced?

The first time my son looked like he was headed in the wrong direction, I took him to talk with his uncle, who had been to jail, so that he could hear from the mouth of experience. I didn't leave him to his own experiments about crime and the law.

By the time a man looks back at where he came from, he is about 50% of the man he could be. I say 50% because he did not know that he could get to this point of his life on purpose. Instead, life's pitfalls and setbacks have forced him to redirect and become who he is today. If he adds a wife and children to his life, they are simply along for the ride.

Because of the lack of fulfillment in our early years, we kind of "learn as you go" with our family and finances, making unnecessary mistakes along the way.

Ladies, if you have a son and you do not want him to struggle like you see the men you are complaining about struggle, then you have to ask yourself: Are you really doing the next woman a favor or giving her just the shaft? Men, are you really modeling what you want your sons to be, even if you must put your life on hold?

There is no getting around the fact that we are all responsible for tomorrow. If you want to know why your spouse is jacked up, look up their family tree. We are products of our immediate family, not people who lived 400 years ago.

THE MAN IN ME

The man in me cries often, from the pain of not being loved to the inability to love to finally starting to love myself and knowing that my children need to feel my love and reciprocate it as well. Cry if you feel like it; it does wonders.

I knew what I had to do, and it came so clearly right when I was going to take my own life. See, the man in us feels underdeveloped, cheated, angry, and confused about our role. The people we draw into our lives have expectations of what we should be. Ignorance of our role does not get a pass from the women we choose to have in our lives or the children that look to us to lead them. I get it now: I am the alpha and the omega of my seed. They draw strength from my walk; they mimic what I do; and they hurt when I hurt.

The man in me says I have no option but to get my act together. I have to learn for the sake of those I have been placed in charge of. Never give an excuse when you can seek and find an answer so their lives can be fuller. The tough part of breaking through my own pain and shame is over for me. The wrenching step to addressing my old pains and family shortcomings is no longer a brick wall. I purposely put my pain aside to make sure my children were no longer in pain so I could help them grow through me because I was not strong enough to do it for myself. I also grew to understand that my family needed love as much as they needed my modeling and guidance. I could not look for excuses for situations and circumstances I created at this point in my life. I had to arrest my decision-making process to learn how to generate long-term solutions and not the feel-good "Jiffy Mix" fixes that have often come back to haunt me later. The man in me has transformed into the dad I should be.

It's hard to convey this to other men because most are not seeing the bigger picture… yet. When they wake up, they will realize where they went wrong and seek the inner strength to change their lives and the lives they created. I am nothing special, and what I am doing does not make me a super dad. I am just getting my family back on track to where it should be.

I am living my best life because I am not afraid to change the direction of my life. I bravely admit to myself that I was not whole in my role as a husband and father, and I will fix it. I'm excited about what I can do since I am now awake. My goal in life is to help other males become the men they silently crave to be and the men their families hope and pray for them to be as well.

WHAT IS A REAL MAN?

The biggest flaw is that we are not on the same page when it comes to defining anything. Damn what Webster's Dictionary says.

Many people will tell you their version of what a real man is. We can spend thousands of words on social media trying to come up with one agreeable statement. I think it boils down to three major characteristics, and many sub-traits can be derived from them.

Three major traits:

- **Accountability**

- **Responsibility**

- **Limitations**

Accountability: the quality or state of being *accountable*; an obligation or willingness to accept responsibility or to account for one's actions, e.g., public officials lacking *accountability*.

Responsibility: the quality or state of being *responsible,* such as moral, legal, or mental accountability; reliability or trustworthiness. It is something for which one is *responsible,* e.g., he has neglected his *responsibilities*.

Limitations: an act or instance of limiting; the quality or state of being limited; something that *limits*; a restraint.

These are the traits we are honing right now in our forties and fifties. However, there is no age requirement for these traits to be taught and practiced **before** our children leave home. These traits are super important in every aspect of their adult lives. Unfortunately, they are learning these lessons through failure after failure.

Example: Most young people have no clue about finances, yet as a parent, you pay bills, monitor your credit, and maintain a home. Why are these the things that most children fail at after leaving home? Even worse, these are events that take place daily in every home.

Who is in charge of sharing that information? More importantly, why are we not creating some type of practical application before the child leaves home? If you want them to succeed, you have to train them to succeed. We need to stop thinking that suffering is at the forefront of learning a lesson. It is the last resort for a child after they fail to apply what they were taught.

One of the worst things I heard was, "I got mine; you

better get yours." The big issue with that statement is trying to define what is **"yours."**

Your man-child isn't a mind reader and doesn't come with instructions. The only thing you have is a list of what you got from your parents and what you found out on your own.

Wanting love from a parent is instinctive. The flow of love and the difference between good and bad love depend on what is shared and displayed in front of the child. Parents do not seem to grasp that they are responsible for that. Everything matters to your child, from who you choose as a partner to how you interact with them to how and why you must end relationships. Men who have no clue about this area make way too many mistakes. They hurt people as part of their journey to learn about themselves.

The clear issue seems to be that we were not made on purpose most of the time, so we were not loved and educated on purpose or to the best of our abilities. If that were not the case, then why are there so many lost children wandering around? Evolution should take place from generation to generation on purpose and without hesitation, not after our sons have been pushed into the system, their freedom is gone and, most of the time, they lose hope altogether.

For the sake of not arguing with "yesterday," we may have to start anew with what a real man is. For years, we have struggled with the concept. It has been graded on a curve and kicked in the groin a few times. Let's say what it is not first because we tend to be drawn to the negative first. It is not how macho, angry, or egotistical a male can be. We've been running on the fumes of anger for years, screaming, "I'm a grown-ass man!" However, you are not doing grown-man stuff. This may seem a little out of reach to some, but if you truly want the fruits of being a real man, you are going to have to start living like one.

I knew the type of man I wanted to be but had no clue how to become him. I had to imagine what that person would do in almost every situation. In my book, "When You Wake up," I describe how, during my purposeful transformation, I questioned every decision I made for eight straight months. By 2008, my moral compass was just spinning with no sense of direction. It wasn't until 2011 that I purposely started. I reflected all the way down to my DNA, aka "pull my head out of my ass," to understand where I was and where I wanted to go. So, here are the things I had to grasp to stop failing myself.

Stop being angry at the world. I know the world uses anger against the black man. It should not be your "go-to" feeling.

Say what you feel. Too many years of suppressing my feelings, erupting on my family, and fighting strangers had taken their toll.

Figure out what is really hurting. Pain makes a man lash out, even at those who love him. We need to know why the pain occurred and, sometimes, who caused it.

Be honest with yourself. There are way too many times

when you don't want to accept the truth right in front of your face.

Locate a decision-making core. Learn to make long-term decisions based on what is right, rather than what feels good or relieves temporary pain.

You cannot lead your life through guilt. Do not do things because you failed in another area.

Address your pain. It is one thing to know why you are hurt, but you also have to attempt to confront it.

Connect with your family. Quite often, there are other family members just as hurt as you are, and some of them need your strength to grow.

Stop having fruitless relationships. Sex is not medicine, nor is it pillow counseling. While you are trying to sex your way to love, someone is falling in love with you, which makes life even messier.

Misery loves company. Do not be afraid to pull back from your toxic friendships with "they get me" kind of friends. There is a good chance they are in the same hurt locker as you, but no one is looking for the latch to get out.

Two things to beware of are religion and drugs or alcohol. They both mask the work you need to do. Neither one will answer your questions, which only you can answer. Religion and alcohol or drugs will be there later; you need a real time out. Just pray for strength and keep it moving.

Seek help. Many men have gone on this journey, and they are there to help. No man should be an island.

Try to fix what you have broken. Ownership of your choices is important. It hurts to start, but it does get better for you and those you hurt or let down.

Set personal goals to measure your life. Without goals and milestones, you cannot see your progress.

Love the ones you made. If you have children, open your heart to them. They need your love; it's not going to be a party, but it will get better the more you engage them. They need healing too.

By now you have noticed I'm not sharing the traditional stuff you always hear about what we need to adhere to. That's because most of that stuff does not cut deep enough to sustain change.

Honesty, trustworthiness, and integrity—all those things are byproducts of clearing your head and jump-starting self-care. The common theme is to get yourself together, and many in your life can and will benefit from your efforts.

Our lack of love and education has brought us exactly where we are today. We do not even trust the help that is offered for free, simply because those who made us failed us.

The Real Man is waiting inside for you to connect and be let out. You need to get away from that aching feeling that makes you slow to change. I did not know I had it in me. I was a Marine for twenty-three years, leading men and traveling the world as an old-ass boy. But I could not see exactly where I stood as a man, a husband, or a father.

Before you say you are a grown-ass man again, make sure you are doing grown-man stuff. Once you start doing that, the young men in your charge will follow your lead.

What is Whole?

Being whole has nothing to do with being in a relationship; I'm sorry if that spoils it for you. Wholeness should come before you select a wife and start having children. In a perfect world, that would be our Method of Operation (MO). Unfortunately, our current MO is to connect with someone who is less or equally jacked up as we are. Another reason could be selecting people with the potential for financial stability or producing a child who will be the next Michael Jordan or Lebron James.

When we choose people too early, it makes us subject to being a passenger on their "Pain Train," which they very well have no clue they are on themselves. Being considered "whole" means you have addressed areas in your life and put everything where it needs to be. I have found that it is our past that keeps us from being whole, which creates the fear of change or the lack of awareness that change needs to take place. To move towards wholeness, a few steps need to be taken.

First, recognize where you came from.

Second, acknowledge how you feel today.

Third, do something about it.

Fourth, redefine your life.

Quite often, I think a good majority of people are stuck between steps and haven't been hurt enough to move to the next step. It's so sad that we are only inspired by pain or loss.

RECOGNIZE WHERE YOU COME FROM

A huge portion of the unaddressed issues in our lives come from our childhood. I know by now you are starting to notice that your tales of your childhood are not unique. We're starting to read book after book and testimony after testimony which all sound very similar. The things you went through as a child, whether it was molestation, neglect, or emotional abuse, all affect how you will deal with life as an adult. In your nightmares, you could be anti-social or lack the ability to love altogether. The pain and shame of yesterday carry a lot of weight. This is even before venturing out into the world and starting new relationships with other people. At times, we do not know how it affects us until we are in relationships.

Clearly, we know by now that women who were mistreated and suffered from an absent father have issues. **News Flash!** The same goes for men who were not connected to or were abused by their mothers. You are living your life based on bad data and pain. The things that you went through have skewed your vision of how life, family, and love should go. You may not be able to see it, but if you ask people who have been in relationships with you, they can give you a little bit of insight into your behavior and emotional aches and pains.

Only you can visit that place in your head to see and replay your life and feelings. You cannot keep hiding those feelings because they have a way of seeping out into other areas of your life, whether it's your ability to love or how you raise your children.

ACKNOWLEDGE HOW YOU FEEL TODAY

Our past can easily be like cancer, and if it's never treated, it can one day kill everything we love. You must openly speak about it and how it made you feel. Surrendering to a feeling that has been buried for years can and will be traumatic. I personally did not stop and look at my life until I was forty-plus years old, a dad, and going through a divorce. I was not able to put my finger on my "why." The "why" is your core reason for why or how you conduct yourself in life with your family, friends, and even your co-workers.

There are so many things you do today because of yesterday that often restrict the way you love and make it hard for people to love you.

Some examples of these are:

- People who often come across as rude

- "Blunt force trauma" when engaging in conversation

- Parents who seem extremely overprotective of their children

- Prejudice against people of the opposite sex

- Abandonment issues that automatically drive people away

- Arguing and fighting to resolve issues with family, a mate, or a spouse

You are conducting your life based on what you went through, and everyone around you hears, sees, and feels it.

DO SOMETHING ABOUT IT

There are many options for what can be done, but doing nothing and expecting everyone to accept your tainted ways is no longer an option because your children are sponges. Either they will mimic your ways or reject your love. Remember what I said earlier—we have lived long enough to know this is true. Seeking help outside our normal remedies—sex, drugs, violence, and ignoring our negative impact on our children—is no longer an option. We cannot keep asking, "What is wrong with the kids of today?" We are what is wrong with the children of today: years of hoarding old pain and blindly letting our childhood parents parent our children today, or the lack of parenting taking place because we were abandoned or left to be raised by our extended families. There is no more "Taboo" to getting professional help. If you think your seed is just going to grow beyond your painful parenting or lack of parenting at all, you will have to do something you've never done. Just remember that this is what those who made you should have thought about in your upbringing. You must change on purpose, not after your children are hurtful and rebellious to you because they figured out that you were not the best parent you could be.

We have a flaw; it's the thought that we are entitled to love, and we will keep going back to our parents seeking that love when even they cannot love themselves and are too hurt to change their ways. We cannot keep waiting for them to wake up. You have to be the cycle-breaker and the maker of tomorrow's history. Seeking help today is the most powerful gift you can give your children to ensure your bloodline evolves in a positive direction.

REDEFINE YOUR LIFE

This is the coolest part of the journey; you get to love, laugh, define who you want to be and what direction you want to go, and take a few people with you. The years of hiding and coping with pain, living with neglect, and even feeling shame have taken you away from who you might have thought you were going to be. Maybe you cried silently and wished your life was different, to the point where you wished you were someone else or in a different family. At this point in your life, you can lift that 1,000-pound weight off your chest, and you can make the changes to be that person, that parent, and that husband you always wanted to be. It's been three years for me, after purposely entering my therapist's office seeking guidance and almost getting permission to accept the hand that was dealt to me by way of my family and what took place while in the Marines. I never knew I could make changes in my life within days. I did not know I could make an impact in my children's lives by getting my act together. I know it now, and I love it.

Men, you are so important to so many people. You have been too hurt and emotionally defeated to see it. I cannot put into words how excited I am about the freedom and mental room I possess in my head to change my life.

The only downside is that not everyone in your life or circle wants you to change. Some of them might have adapted to the 50 and 75% Man, and if you change, that means they will have to change as well or be left behind.

The greatest fear that you will have is that if you are connected to and have built a life with a 75% Woman and she is not ready for her journey, then your relationship could be in jeopardy.

Your journey towards being the best you that you could be will bring you closer to peace; the closer you are to peace, the more you will be able to sidestep chaos in your path. It is almost like a superpower. Don't you want to be a superhero?

THE BEGINNING

When this book came to me in my dreams, I was setting out to answer what is wrong with the men of today. I was so tired of women complaining about us. The bottom line is that the systematic division of the black family has worked. We cannot see beyond our pain to correct the course. We all have to take a step back and look at where we are today and, as a whole, decide where we want to be tomorrow. Our issue is no longer political or economic; it is our lack of unity. Cultural unity will solve 80% of our current issues. We must want it together. Read the Bonus Book "The Living Solution," because, at this point, we have no choice but to solve our problems ourselves.

Be Powerful

BONUS BOOK:

THE LIVING SOLUTION

TABLE OF CONTENTS

Preface 33

The Five-Step Process 35

Identify the Problem 36

Who or What Caused the Problem? 38

Solve the Problem 40

What is the Lesson Learned? 43

Rules to Live By 45

What is our Problem? 47

Who Caused the Problem? 51

How Can We Fix It? 53

Our Lessons Learned 57

Life Rules 59

The Distractions 63

The Big Picture 67

PREFACE

We have a problem that has been brewing for decades and has become our norm. A good number of our youth are in a tailspin. They are hurt and lost in a fog of pain. Most parents are living with hidden pain as well. Many of them are numb and unable to love their own children. I think people are confused about what our true problem is. We, as a culture, are hiding in religion, distracted by the media, and angry at politicians. Our focus has been on the symptoms we see and not the core of our problem, which is the deterioration of the family. Our nation spends millions of our tax dollars on the symptoms and not the reeducation of the family. Even worse, the families do not self-educate about this problem. However, we can fix this.

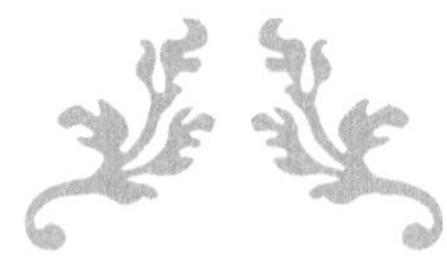

THE FIVE-STEP PROCESS

I think as a person grows, they systematically develop their own approach to solving problems. This may require a lot of trial and error, and each person will learn to grasp the concept of how to solve problems at various stages of their life. They also have to be able to articulate this skill to their children. Once a person masters the concept, their life becomes simpler. In that way, they find themselves functioning with less stress, and they are happier in life. This will require a person to practice their problem-solving skills until they have an automatic response when an issue presents itself.

I have been the "battery" in my family for more than twenty years. (A full definition of the role of a battery is in my book, "Batteries and Suckers"). In short, I solve problems, and it has become my primary role in my family. They call me to help create a solution to a problem or help them map out a new idea. Over the years, I have seen many problems that people deal with, as well as my own. I began to understand that I had a pattern for approaching a problem, and it became second nature. If you have not developed your own problem-solving template, I am more than happy to share mine.

The steps listed below are things I have asked myself while attempting to solve an issue. Over time, the one thing I had to remove from the process was how I felt. Emotions do not solve problems; sometimes, they make things worse. Therefore, most feelings should be put aside while formulating a plan. It is not that I do not want to feel the emotion, but some problems are time-sensitive, and the solution needs to come as soon as possible.

The five steps to solving a problem are:

- Identify the problem.

- Who or what caused the problem?

- Solve the problem.

- What are the lessons learned?

- Generate a new life rule.

IDENTIFY THE PROBLEM

Identifying a problem should involve a deep look at everything and everyone that could be affected by the problem and the long-term consequences if the problem has not been resolved. A problem is something that will slow down or stop your overall plan from succeeding.

Quite often, a lack of money is a problem. Some general reasons for money problems are:

- Theft

- Loss of Job

- Lack of Work

- Overspending

- Old Bills

- New Bills

The key to solving the problem is to identify how it came to be in the first place. Problems left uncorrected do not simply fade away. They tend to have the shelf life of a can of spam. It is important to assess the problem without emotions and begin the process. I'm not saying you cannot express your sense of loss or frustration. However, your ability to attack the problem as soon as possible will reduce most of those feelings.

People will say problems are a part of life, but the key to a simple life is how you respond to problems. Not every problem can be resolved in a day, but the quicker the solution is drawn up, the quicker you can get back to your scheduled plan.

Example:

You lend money to a friend, and they swear they are going to pay you back on their next payday, which is right around rent time. You and the friend utilize the same bank, and the friend says they will put the money in your account by the first of the month. One week later, your rent is due; you write the check as you always have on the first of the month. On the fifth of the month, you get a letter from the property office stating that your rent is late. On the same day, the bank sends you a text stating that your account is overdrawn. Now you have a compound problem. The core of the problem is that you trusted someone with enough money that without their repayment, your whole budget could be thrown off. The result of your choice to lend the money is late payment for the rent and overdraft charges from the bank, not to mention the unpaid money from your friend or should I say, your ex-friend.

WHO OR WHAT CAUSED THE PROBLEM?

When it comes down to who caused the problem, it is important not to falsely blame the wrong person. Wrongly accusing people of a problem only makes things worse. Quite often, this happens when a person is emotionally charged about what has failed them.

When it comes down to who caused the problem in the process, it helps to look beyond the usual suspects to see the bigger picture. In the case of theft, sometimes things really come out in the wash. On a few of my laundry days, I found more than fifty dollars in the dryer. I could have easily blamed others for my missing money. Identifying the right person and going over how the problem came to be is very important for the future.

When assessing the problem, look for two things:

malice and mistakes. When a person does something against you or your plan intentionally, it can be said or done out of malice. There is no room for these negative acts in your life, and you have to decide whether you want to move forward with the relationship or stop it right there.

When a mistake ignites a problem, there isn't much to do but attempt to make sure that it does not happen again. What are the possible unforeseen things that may cause a problem?

Some causes of problems are:

- Usual wear and tear

- Natural disasters or weather

- Change in laws

- Expirations date

- Poor workmanship

- Ignorance

Either way, it is important to investigate all the possible reasons why your plan or goal was interrupted. This is done to protect your time, money, and family in the future.

SOLVE THE PROBLEM

No one knows everything, but having a strong list of resources helps provide a solution to a problem.

Some resources are:

- Internet

- Books and manuals

- Manufacturers

- Blogs

- Family members

- Strangers

I have had much success with the internet. Over time, I have found that there are many sources on the internet to visit, including the following:

YouTube: Watching videos on the subject is very helpful. However, I recommend watching at least three different providers on the subject to look for slight differences. One person may be using a special tool designed by the manufacturer, and another person may use a common household tool to fix the same item. When it comes to learning a new technique, YouTube has scores and scores of free classes.

Books and manuals: These are often available to download off the internet. Some are free, and there are a few times you might have to pay for one. I make it a habit not to throw away books or items I have purchased. Reading the literature before attempting to repair an item helps and can save you from making more mistakes.

Manufacturers: Manufacturer websites are a great place to start when you are working on items. Here you can find, and recall information and any free fixes that a company may offer. Today, most manufacturers place their videos on YouTube for their customers to make it simpler to solve common issues with their products.

Blogs: Blogs and enthusiast websites are very good for those hard-to-find answers. Blogging is a running conversation in which many readers share their perspectives on a particular topic. Once, I could not find a fix for my car not starting. I tried all the things I mentioned above, but there was no solution available. I began to search blog topics about my issue and found my answer. It was in a sentence at the end of a thread, but it was just what I needed to get the job done.

Family Members: We often forget about the wealth of knowledge our family possesses. I think it is important to know what your family members do for a living. It could be from doctors to landscapers. I took a survey of the jobs in my family and found out we had at least six members working in the medical field. It is always nice to have that go-to mechanic in the family as well. Elders in the family may not have the skills that apply to today's industries, but some possess unique problem-solving skills that were tested over time.

Strangers: When all else fails, ask a stranger. I have gotten a lot of good information from people I did not know. Because you never know who has the solution to your problem, I'm never afraid to strike up a conversation with someone I do not know.

Once I had a car problem while driving from Washington state to Indiana, and I could not find a solution. The issue forced me to pull over to the side of the road every three hours on my road trip and sit for at least ten minutes each time. After some time had passed, I could start the car and continue my journey. I had stopped at least three mechanic's shops along the way, and no one had the answer. I was at my wit's end by the time I made it to Indiana. Just before I made it to my house, I stopped at a gas station to top off my tank. The gas station had no service department, not even an air pump. An older man was sitting on a milk crate. I walked over to him and said, "I have a problem with my car, and I will tell you my story. I think you may have the answer." I completed the tale of trials and tribulations I had with the car. The man rubbed his chin for about ten seconds and then told me the most profound thing: "Take the car home and drop the gas tank. Once you get it on the ground, remove the flow from the tank, and clean the strainer, then your car will be fine." I did just that, and that fixed my car. I learned not to count out unexpected help; it was right on time.

The speed of solving vs. planning a long-term solution is a huge factor. The speed of fixing a problem depends on many variables:

- Time

- Resources available

- Skill set

- Willingness to solve the problem

At this point in the process, we have to pick a course of action based on the items listed above. Determining which route to take is very important; this is where experience and a person's ability to think outside the box are important. We cannot fix everything with a hammer, nor can we just wish a problem away. This is why I recommend enlisting the help of an elder or someone who has dealt with a similar problem in the past. They might have made several different attempts before they found the right fix for the problem—fixes you may not need to attempt.

WHAT IS THE LESSON LEARNED?

People are always quoting the old cliché, "You live, and you learn." I think this cliché is outdated and needs an upgrade. "You live, you learn, and then you apply what you learn," is better. Far too often, I see people relearning the same lessons. Whether it is in their own lives or lessons, we can see it in other people's lives. Some lessons are very costly to the person and their family.

Great Example:

I am pretty sure that everyone knows how devastating the use of crack is to the body, mind, and family. There are movies, songs, and jokes made about this drug. Millions of families have been torn apart, not to mention the generational damage. I beg for the answer: why do we still have people trying this drug for the first time in this day and age? There is no logical reason, yet people are still throwing their families into harm's way.

There are free lessons everywhere, yet we, as human

beings, tend to dredge the same path of failure as many have done before us. It is often said, "Doing the same thing over and over and expecting a different outcome is a sign of insanity." I think this could be said about people who repeat the same failures as those before them as well. There is no patent on the life lessons that people have already learned. I believe the family hierarchy is designed for elders to pass down wisdom to the next generation to create a stronger and smarter bloodline, as I explained in my book "Batteries and Suckers."

We must retain the life lessons to save time, money, and the loss of life by training anyone and everyone in our lives to ensure we move forward as a people. We must embrace this concept as the standard for family learning.

When solving a problem, you must openly state what the lesson learned was, or you are bound to repeat it. As clearly stated in the cliché, "a man who does not know his history is doomed to repeat it." We often hear this shared by people who peddle historical information about our Black History. However, this can be said about our recent history to help educate our immediate family by sharing life lessons we have already learned.

Great Example:

A man decides he wants to be the neighborhood drug dealer and leads a life of crime. He is shot at, incarcerated, and removed from his family and his children. We often see his children following in their father's footsteps. Now we have two generations behind bars, and the family suffers even more.

Many lessons can be learned from this including the following:

1. Selling drugs has the potential for death.

2. As a result of your example, your children will mimic your actions.

3. You can ruin your bloodline.

4. Modeling is important in a child's life.

5. All of the above.

This lesson does not require any further research. Crack has plagued our community for decades; we know the outcome. We are recycling a lesson that should have died in prison years ago.

RULES TO LIVE BY

Much of my success has come from establishing Life Rules. A life rule comes from lessons I've personally learned or something I've seen others go through. I mean, why not let the world be your dummy? At this point in our lives, there is barely anything you could fail at that someone has not shared in a book, movie, or even with your neighbor. Life rules breed peace in your life. Without rules, there is chaos, and many of us have found complacency in that already.

When a rule is established, it is to protect my family, money, property, and health. Life rules can stop us from learning the same lessons over and over.

Some Life Rules are:

- Do not use drugs.

- Do not text and drive.

- Do not drink and drive.

- Keep guns out of reach of children.

- Never lend money to broke people.

- Do not lend your car to those who cannot replace it or do not have the deductible.

I have been following these steps at a snail's pace for the last ten years. I have soaked up lessons from smart people, not-so-smart people, people who have succeeded in life, and some who have failed. I just wanted to make my life simple so that my children do not have to reinvent the wheel to find peace in their lives.

The five steps I have shared can help streamline many of the issues that appear in our day-to-day lives. But I think we can use it on a bigger scale. Let's look at our problem.

WHAT IS OUR PROBLEM?

Our problem is complex because, over time, our eyes have been trained to look at and treat our symptoms.

Some symptoms are:

- Black on Black Crime

- School dropouts

- Drug usage

- Excessive use of government aid

- High unemployment rate

Yes, these are huge problems as they stand alone, but as they are all going on at the same time, there just may be a bigger problem that is feeding into these symptoms. The problem we have is pretty much on automatic pilot at this point.

I see more and more books on how this problem began and how steps were taken to ensure that the control of the masses would be kept covertly in place behind the scenes through laws and bills. To some, this was a plan, but to the people who are suffering, it is a problem.

It is no secret that the decline of the family was the plan and was thoroughly orchestrated to ensure that one race would remain at the top of the food chain. For many generations before me, this was the plan and scheme. I must say the plan has worked brilliantly.

My issue with the problem we face is that we are so comfortable planning our demise that we cannot come together to solve it.

The decline of the family is the root cause. The disease of dysfunction is the poison behind all the symptoms listed earlier. I also believe that using our tax dollars to massage this problem has created a monster that can barely be contained.

I am no scholar; I am but a simple man with a small degree in business management. I do not have political ties or a huge religious background. What I do possess is common sense, and when I have applied it in the last few years, it has resulted in changes in my life that have affected everyone around me. The result of my change has moved my life to a place of peace and a need to see others in peace as well.

The decline in the family is a mix of shame and pain from poor decision-making that often results in the birth of a child—children that no one planned for and had no clue how to raise. I often hear, "They did the best they could with what they had." I can understand that in my grandparents' time. My parents were a product of that upbringing, so they get a semi-pass. As we have grown into the age of technology and the retention of data, I find it hard to give a pass to those who were born after 1965. At some point, the lack of tools, modeling, and love is no longer an excuse.

WHO CAUSED THE PROBLEM?

We are now down to who caused the problem. Generations of lawmakers geared to keep our culture down. Was it Willie Lynch who created the book that was a cornerstone in the decimation of Black Culture? Was it the hateful people who continue to pass down hate to their seed and train them to follow the old belief that blacks are inferior? These are the elements that started decades ago. The grip they had on our culture was choking the very life out of our families.

I cannot leave out the very people who had the power to attempt to reunite the family—black people who had control over the day-to-day teaching and raising of our solution. By 1965, we truly understood the laws and bills that were in place to crush our will. Broken parents dealing with severe family dysfunction and living in the fog of pain have a lot to do with it.

I noticed that not every child was raised in a fog of dysfunction. Not every young girl was molested, and not every son was beaten regularly. Some parents continued the cycle of pain and handed it down to their children without knowing that it did not have to be like that.

Some would say we cannot hold our parents responsible because of how they were raised. I find it hard not to hold them responsible for the lack of love in their home after they had children. The government does not control the amount of love that can be given to a child. Nor does it regulate what you can teach your child in your home. Hugs and kisses do not have a ceiling cap that limits the parents. Teaching your children how to conduct their lives and giving them skills to help them survive once they leave the fold is not forbidden. No one seems to want to point a finger at who is directly responsible for the children.

We cannot ignore the fact that some parents have mentally checked out because of the pain they suffered during their lives with their parents. Which brings up the question: how could you not want a better life for your child? How does a parent not seek to make their seed greater than themselves? I see parents screaming as their child is shot in the streets and spends years in prison, but the cardinal training and love that tend to prevent that negative behavior and the feeling of being "unloved" were in the parents' hands and under their charge.

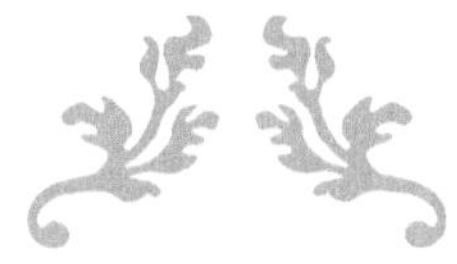

How Can We Fix It?

I have watched millions and millions of dollars put into programs and systems to help with our cultural issues. At this point, they are only treating our symptoms. There are not enough programs reeducating the part of the family that is responsible for loving and educating the children. Some parents have no clue what parenting means. Many are too hurt to seek help to be better than their parents. We often share the statement, "It was not modeled for us." "No one ever showed me love; how can I show my child?" There is enough data on parenting and real, loving families to get a new idea of what positive parenting can create.

The biggest piece to fixing this issue is to redefine our roles as parents and educate our young parents in skills that will improve their lives and the lives of their children after them.

Great Example:

Young parents struggle with understanding what credit is and how important it is to get it under control as soon as possible. Why? It's because the average young person accumulates negative credit by age twenty due to their failure to understand financial responsibility, which results in their being unable to obtain affordable housing, dealing with high-interest rates on cars, and having a lack of buying power. I did not master many of these things until I was well into my late thirties because I was not taught about money before I left home.

Children tend to stumble around for years when their parents do not invest in their future. Either they never get a handle on it, or the child is so emotionally damaged that they become emotionally deaf.

We need to make greater children. We give them cars and freedom, not responsibilities. Many have no understanding of love and family. Children are forced to leave home empty-handed or run from home as soon as they see the door open. We need to stop letting our children learn by trial and error because we know the outcome.

Instead of overtly teaching and loving them to prepare them to champion their bloodline, we see the jails filled with young people who only knew violence and took what they needed by force. Parenting is a process of handing down knowledge to our children, teaching them good things, and warning them of bad things they may encounter after they leave the nest.

Of course, this sounds too simple to be true. Yes, it is easier said than done, but many have not tried it yet. Giving program assistance without training is a mess. It is patchwork instead of solving the real issue. I see hundreds of books showing how we got to this point. What I don't see are real programs for the education of the family—no programs that poke the elephant in the room. We must pull families out of the fog of dysfunction. It is too hard to point out the core of dysfunction in each family from the outside.

However, once the awakening happens, the pit of pain and shame will be exposed. People say this is not a good time to fix a family's broken heart. But waiting for the elder to tell the truth on their deathbed is a bit late. There is never a good time but now sounds great. We have very little time to turn this around. We have been treating the wrong thing for years.

How can you say Willie Lynch's book is a direct cause and we have not been teaching the direct opposite for the past forty years? I think that because it has run its course for so long, not being unified has become our norm. We have embraced coping skills but not problem-solving skills. We have not found a way to hold individual families responsible for the children they let out into the world to suffer due to a lack of love and home training.

Why tackle family dysfunction? Because it produces hurt and incomplete people, and those incomplete people become the parents of tomorrow. They hurt more people, and so on and so forth. I am not a psychologist, but it doesn't take three degrees to see the issue. Or is it just where we are supposed to be? Because if our children were loved, cared for, and educated on how to function as young adults, get jobs, and create a cycle of making greater children, this world would not be the same as we see in the news today.

"Better parents make better children; they make better parents, then they make better children." N2P

Do you have a better plan?

Families are treating dysfunction like bad credit. "I can just wait until it falls off," but it doesn't work that way with people.

Bottom Line:

I feel the only way to fix this problem is to make better children. Better children will make better parents. We need to create a new cycle from this point on. The children will be equipped with the wisdom of the lessons that have already been paid for by their parents and grandparents. We must start with the family unit and make sure they have the best environment inside the home.

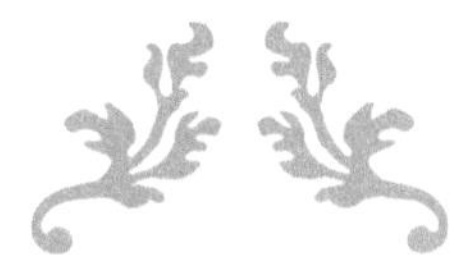

OUR LESSONS LEARNED

So, what have we learned? Again, six years of college are not needed to learn a lesson. Here are a few lessons learned:

1. Silence of child molestation and abuse, hurt children, and they turn into hurt adults.

2. Unloved children have a greater chance of being killed or jailed.

3. We are scared to kick the elephant out of the house.

4. We send our children out into the world unarmed with no skills and spend more years recovering than moving forward.

5. We value shame and pride over love.

6. We can't wait for other cultures to save us.

7. We are thoroughly distracted.

8. We do not teach family love.

I'm sure you can list many lessons yourself. If you see what I see, then why are we waiting, or better yet, what are we waiting on to fix our families? There are scores of lessons learned over the last five decades. Even worse, society has created programs to deal with those lessons we fail to eradicate. In this new history, we have a chance to use all resources to our advantage, but many of us are still stuck. Why?

LIFE RULES

To not repeat old lessons, you should generate a list of things in which you will not participate in the future because you already know the outcome. Why reinvent the wheel? For the problems and lessons I have seen in our culture, I have created a simple list that helps me to govern my family and create a place of peace.

- Family unity is necessary to make better children.

- Do not use or sell drugs.

- Research things that are given away for free.

- For every problem, find a solution and share it.

- List your goals and never be distracted from the bigger picture.

- Be a lawmaker, not a lawbreaker.

- Educate yourself and others when you can.

You are responsible for what enters your life. The life rules you create symbolize what you have already learned. Some people want you to bend the rules—not for you, but for them. Let that sink in. You already learned the lesson; they want you to go against what others have already learned. When you say to yourself, "I knew it, I knew it," about the outcome of a situation, you have repeated something that has already been learned. That means the price of the lesson has doubled. Normally, it takes a person a lifetime to make these rules for themselves. The sooner you learn the art of rulemaking, the smoother your life will be. We must find ways to evolve without losing life, money, or friendship, to name a few.

For myself, I have a list of rules:

- Lending money creates bad blood. It is better to give it away, but only if you can afford to.

- Never trust someone with something you cannot afford to lose.

- Getting high is not for me, and no one can tell me differently.

- Help people until they show you they want to fail, and then let them fail.

- It's okay to complain, but having a solution to go with it is greater.

- Do not want someone who doesn't want you.

- Teach people how to fish, and they will either leave

you alone or grow.

- Tell people that you have reached your limit of listening to chaos and problems.

- Tell people how you feel so you do not suffer in silence.

This is not a perfect science, but I have found that many people do not have a system and often freeze in place until help comes. By the time help arrives, they have created a new problem on top of the previous one. Our problem requires a long-term solution; there is no quick fix. So, we need to get to work on individual solutions, which in turn will solve many of our bigger issues as a culture. As I stated, I'm a simple man, and I feel that many of our lessons have been learned. The problem is we cannot seem to come together and apply the needed solutions that we can control inside our homes, and that directly affects our community. I mean, that is our goal, right?

THE DISTRACTIONS

There are many things we encounter today that I feel distract us from moving forward.

Some distractions are:

- American Greed

- Politics

- Religion

- Old pain and shame

- Fear of change

American greed and the need for material things above family unity are problems. We are more interested in what we want than we are in protecting what we have. The family is a living thing; it thinks, feels, hurts, and sometimes does amazing things. When you put material things first, like buying a home you cannot afford or a car to show off to your peers, and do not properly prepare to finance a family, you are creating a problem that will affect everyone in the family.

Politics can and has divided homes. The views outside the home should not affect how you love and teach your children. The core values of the family do not come from politics. How much you love your child or wife does not come from the polls. As parents, you must govern to teach and maximize the growth of your seed. Letting outsiders divide your family is what family should stand against; if anything, it should bring you closer. Most cultures do not fail to be a family because of a change in administration.

Religion has been around for a long time. Some families have belonged to churches since the doors opened. I fail to see, on a large scale, how religion has become a part of the solution. Yes, they share guidelines according to the Bible. Yes, they teach the power of prayer. How is it that they do very little but take in money from those families who need help and do not generate programs in the same community to move families forward? They can do more, and we should demand more from our religion.

Old pain and shame are a huge part of the stagnant movement of the redirection of the family. Family dysfunction is at the core of our issues. Some elders have run their families into the ground because of something that happened to them as children. Even worse is that some cannot bring themselves to make the needed changes for their family because of a shameful feeling they have within themselves. Quite often, we will feel we are not worthy of being the change agent, but often you are the only conscious one in the family that knows change must come.

The fear of change will require some exposure, which could come from decisions made years ago and the factors used. How others will view you during the change process may cause a fear of rejection for you or anger from them. Change may require turning a family in a whole new direction. Some may not want the burden of making a better family unit for the reasons I listed above. Remember this: letting the fear of change take over the family kills the family unit.

THE BIG PICTURE

As a family, you must know what you want at the end of the day, whether it is fame, money, peace, unity, or a combination of all of the above. The family goal must be known and embedded in the training and traditions of the family. How else are they going to know? Someone has to sell the family plan to get everyone involved; there is no way around this part. We have been shattered to pieces as a culture, and very few know their family plan, or some are so hurt that they do not care. The big picture is not going to appear overnight, and there needs to be an open discussion about what needs to be changed and worked on to achieve family goals.

To my understanding, we (as a culture) have never openly said we were going to fix our families. Many will not want change, probably because it will hurt so much, and they never thought that healing the family unit will heal them as well. I have seen many solutions, from politics to religion, and feel they have missed the mark time and time again. So, what do we have to lose?

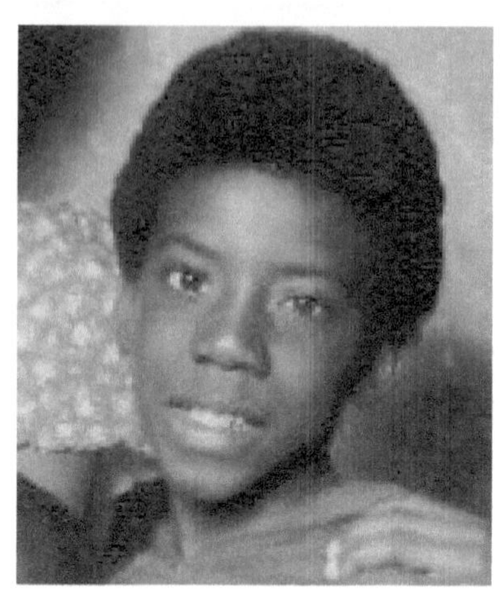

Paul **"Kacky"** Posey

COMING SOON

71

"I am My Own Dad"

I wrote this book to heal myself and to help others begin healing their families. Everyone has a story; some are so similar that it is uncanny. We need to move away from the excuse, "I grew up without a dad." We must sacrifice our pain from yesterday to break the cycle of family dysfunction. Fathers need to find their rightful places in the home and lead their families. I humbly thank God for the guidance of my hand and for accepting my enlistment in the crusade to save our families.